SAMSON

SAMSON

Dan Larsen

© 2013 by Barbour Publishing, Inc.

Written by Dan Larsen. Illustrated by Ken Save.

Print ISBN 978-1-62416-631-0

eBook Editions:
Adobe Digital Edition (.epub) 978-1-62836-285-5
Kindle and MobiPocket Edition (.prc) 978-1-62836-286-2

All rights reserved. No part of this publication may be reproduced or transmitted for commercial purposes, except for brief quotations in printed reviews, without written permission of the publisher.

Churches and other noncommercial interests may reproduce portions of this book without the express written permission of Barbour Publishing, provided that the text does not exceed 500 words and that the text is not material quoted from another publisher. When reproducing text from this book, include the following credit line: "From *Samson*, published by Barbour Publishing, Inc. Used by permission."

All scripture quotations are taken from the King James Version of the Bible.

Cover design: Greg Jackson, Thinkpen Design

Published by Barbour Publishing, Inc., P.O. Box 719, Uhrichsville, Ohio 44683, www.barbourbooks.com

Our mission is to publish and distribute inspirational products offering exceptional value and biblical encouragement to the masses.

Printed in the United States of America.
Offset Paperback Manufacturers, Dallas PA 18612; October 2013;
D10004169

Contents

1. Days of the Judges 7
2. A Surprise Visit 15
3. The Nazirite Vow 23
4. Lion Slayer 33
5. The Riddle 41
6. Fire and Foxes 51
7. The Donkey's Jawbone 59
8. The Power of God 69
9. Betrayed! 77
10. Destruction of Dagon 85
Young Reader's Bible Dictionary 93

Solve the Secret Code!

At the end of each chapter, you'll find a set of numbers—it's the code to a secret message throughout the book.

Each group of four numbers stands for a single letter in the message. Your job is to pinpoint each mystery letter with the codes, then write the letters above each four-digit number group. When you've finished solving each chapter's code, read the letters from chapter one through the end of the book to find out exactly what the secret message says!

Here's how to use the codes:

- The first number is the page number—within that chapter.
- The second number is the paragraph on the page—count full paragraphs only.
- The third number is the word in the appropriate paragraph.
- The fourth number is the letter in the appropriate word—this is the letter you'll write above the number group.

Enjoy the story. . .and solving the secret message!

1
Days of the Judges

It was a dark, dark time for the people of Israel. This was the time before the kings. There was lawlessness. And there were enemies throughout the land.

Many years before, Moses had led the people of Israel out of Egypt and into the desert. God promised His people a land flowing with milk and honey, a land where there would be peace—this land, where they lived now, the land of the Canaanites. God kept His promise.

But those Israelites, under Moses, did not enter here. They had sent out spies into the land of Canaan, and the report had come back: There were giants in the land! There were strong peoples in the land, with iron chariots, mighty in war. And the Israelites were afraid. They did not believe in God's promise to protect them,

Samson

to give them the land. And so God let them go back out into the desert, where all of His unbelieving people lived out the rest of their lives. There they died, and there they were buried in the sand.

It was their children, and their children's children, who would go into this land, the land of milk and honey. Moses had died. The Lord had raised up another leader

for His people. His name was Joshua. He would lead the people across the Jordan River and into the Promised Land. He would lead Israel to victory after victory over the evil nations that were settled in the land.

"Judah must go first," the Lord said. And Judah went into the land and conquered and destroyed. The other tribes of Israel followed and they, too, drove out the evil nations, the godless, and settled in their cities.

But Israel did not drive out all the nations in Canaan, as God had commanded them to do. The Canaanites remained, and the Sidonians, the Hivites, the Philistines, and the Amorites. The Israelites did not capture the cities of Gaza, Ashkelon, or Ekron. The people there had iron chariots. They were strong. And many other cities were left alone—Gezer, Dor, Sidon,

Samson

Rehob, the five cities of the Philistines, and others.

The people of Israel had not obeyed God. But then they sinned even more than this. They settled among these heathen nations and began to worship their gods. They began to serve, especially, the god Baal and the goddess Astarte. And they forgot about their own God, the God of their fathers, the Lord who had rescued them from slavery in Egypt and brought them here to this land. Here the Lord had given His people vineyards they had not had to plant themselves and cities they had not had to build themselves. Here was indeed milk and honey. But here the children of Israel, as their fathers did before them, turned from their Lord and God to other gods and goddesses, idols made of wood and stone and bronze.

And so God let His people have their way. And He let their enemies rule them. There was no peace in the land. The Lord said:

I made you to go up out of Egypt, and have brought you unto the land which I sware unto your fathers; and I said, I will never break my covenant with you. And ye shall make no league with the inhabitants of this land; ye shall throw down their altars: but ye have not obeyed my

Samson

voice: why have ye done this? Wherefore I also said, I will not drive them out from before you; but they shall be as thorns in your sides, and their gods shall be a snare unto you.
JUDGES 2:1–3

The people of Israel had abandoned God. And so God no longer protected them in battle against their enemies. Some of God's people were driven out of their lands. Some were driven out of the plains and up into the hill country.

But at times the people of Israel would remember their God and would cry out to Him. And as He always did whenever His people called to Him, God would answer them. He raised up leaders for His people, who would unite the Israelites and make them strong and lead them in victory against their enemies. And there would be peace—for a time. Then when that leader would die, and Israel would forget, once again, their Lord and God. And then troubles came again to their lands.

In those days they called these leaders "judges." They were not kings. (It was a long time before the days of the kings of Israel.) They were appointed by the Lord Himself to judge and rule His people. There were many of these judges.

There was Othniel, the first, who led Israel in peace for forty years. When he died, there was trouble again in the land. The Moabites rose up against Israel. They

Samson

raided and captured and robbed. Then God gave Israel another judge, Ehud, who defeated Moab, and there was peace in the land for eighty years.

Then it was the Philistines who troubled the Israelites. And God sent one of the greatest judges, a man named Shamgar, to rescue His people. In one battle he killed six hundred Philistines with an ox goad all by himself.

There was Deborah, a prophetess. The Canaanites had ruled Israel with cruelty for twenty years. By the Word of the Lord through Deborah, God chose a leader for Israel, a man called Barak. He broke the power of the Canaanites, and there was peace in Israel for forty years.

Then came the Midianites, who terrorized Israel for seven years. They raided the Israelites' cattle, sheep, and donkeys; they destroyed their vineyards, their wheat, their corn, and their orchards. They stripped the land, and they burned the villages. Israel cried out to God, and God sent them a fearsome man of war, Gideon. With only  three hundred warriors, Gideon defeated thousands of Midianites and drove them from the land, and under Gideon there was peace another forty years.

Samson

There were other judges. Whenever Israel's enemies became too strong for them, Israel would cry out to God, and He would send a judge to deliver them and rule them in peace. Then they would forget and return to their sins and their idols.

And so it went for many, many years.

In the time of this present story, the day of the judges was coming to an end. The day of the kings was near. But before the dark age of the judges closed, there would be one more of these men that God would raise up to strike terror into the enemies of His people. This man, though perhaps not the greatest of these judges, nor even of any man, was, and still is, known as one of the greatest heroes of all time. His feats of strength, his victories, his exploits, though all of them true, have become legend. His name is spoken of with those of the greatest heroes of history.

At the time that God raised up this hero, the Philistines were again troubling Israel. This was one of the nations that the Israelites had not conquered and driven out. The Philistines were a strong people who had settled in the plains to the south and west of the Mediterranean Sea. They had entered this land in the time that the Israelites had gone into the highlands to the north and settled there. The Philistines had captured and now controlled five cities in this land—Gaza, Ashkelon, Ashdod, Ekron, and Gath. They were a wealthy people. Their houses were bigger, richer, and better built than those of the Israelites. The Philistines were well-known for their skill in metalworking. They made copper and iron tools and weapons, and these were coveted around the world.

They had ravaged Asia Minor and had destroyed the Hittite Empire. They had even attacked Egypt, but they did not succeed there. It was after this attempt that they came from the east to overrun and occupy this land, which would become known as the Philistine Plain. The name would become, much later, "Palestine"—this name would come from the name "Philistine."

And it would be these people who would drive Israel to finally cry out to God for a king.

But before Israel's first king, there would be one more judge who would deliver God's people from these enemies, the Philistines. This man had no army. He led no masses into battle. He would work alone. Singlehandedly he would defeat and destroy thousands of Philistines, including the kings of the Philistines' five cities. Singlehandedly he would bring the

Philistines' reign of oppression over Israel to an end and bring peace, for a time, to Israel.

Samson

Secret Code:

$\overline{}$ $\overline{}$ $\overline{}$
5-2-4-1 7-3-5-3 1-1-4-1

$\overline{}$ $\overline{}$ $\overline{}$ $\overline{}$ $\overline{}$ $\overline{}$
3-2-5-3 2-3-7-1 6-2-7-1 1-2-4-5 7-2-3-2 1-3-7-1

$\overline{}$ $\overline{}$ $\overline{}$ $\overline{}$ $\overline{}$ $\overline{}$
5-2-7-1 4-1-6-1 5-1-5-4 2-1-4-4 3-2-4-2 4-4-7-3

2
A Surprise Visit

The Philistines had controlled Israel for forty years. In this part of the country the Israelites and the Philistines lived among one another. The Philistines were a strong nation, as well as rich. They controlled five cities on the southwest coast of the Mediterranean Sea. From here they carried on their sea trade with other parts of the world.

The Israelites in this land were as poor as their Philistine neighbors were rich. Compared with the houses of the Israelites, those of the Philistines were palaces. And the Philistines treated the Israelites, not as neighbors and friends, but as servants and slaves.

There had been no warfare between these two nations yet. The people of Israel had no leaders, no armies. They were scattered tribes of shepherds and farmers—

Samson

tribes that kept to themselves and did not mingle with the others, did not try to unite their forces, to make themselves strong.

Indeed, the Israelites did not feel themselves to be strong enough to stand up to an enemy such as the Philistines. So they went on, year after year after year, suffering their fate in misery. But deep resentment was growing.

On a ridge that looked out over the eastern end of the Valley of Sorek sat a little town called Zorah. This was about a day's journey west from Jerusalem. A man called Manoah, of the tribe of Dan, lived here. His wife was of the tribe of Judah. They had been man and wife for many years, but they had no children.

One afternoon Manoah's wife was in the house alone. Her husband was out working in the fields. She sat in the open doorway in the sunlight, sewing. Suddenly a shadow fell over her. She looked up. Someone was standing in front of her, just outside the door. She had never seen him before.

Indeed, she had never seen anyone like him, ever. He was very tall, and his robe was the whitest she had ever

Samson

seen. There was something else, something about his face. Her hands, she suddenly realized, were shaking. She laid down her sewing. Somehow she felt she must stand before this person. Shakily she got to her feet.

The stranger's voice, though not loud or alarming, made her knees tremble. "Listen to me," the man said. "You have not been able to bear children. Soon you will, though. You will have a son. You must not drink any wine, or any other strong drink, nor must you eat any of the foods that are forbidden to the Lord's people Israel. And after your son is born, you must never cut his hair. Because from the day of his birth he is to be a Nazirite, dedicated to God. He shall begin the work of delivering Israel from the Philistines."

Manoah's wife just stood in the doorway staring at the man's face. She clutched her skirt to keep her hands from shaking. A sense of awe and of fear had come over her as the man spoke. Now she could no longer meet his gaze. She looked down at the floor at her feet. After several moments she looked up, and the man was gone.

She ran out into the fields to where her husband was working. Manoah stopped working when he saw her

Samson

coming. He stood frozen. He had never seen her run like this. And the look on her face...

"Husband!" she said, gasping for breath. "A man of God has come to me!"

"What!" said her husband.

"He...oh, husband, his face! He was like an angel of God."

"What...what did he—?"

"I did not even ask him his name or where he came from. I did not—I could not speak at all. But he told me that I would bear a son and that this boy—our son, husband!—must be dedicated to the Lord from the day of his birth. We must never—his hair must never be cut. And I will—I must, I mean, not drink any wine or other strong drink, or eat any of the forbidden foods. He—our son—is to begin the work of delivering our people—Israel, I mean—from the Philistines!"

Manoah was just staring. His wife never lied. She was not lying now, he knew. He took her gently by the shoulders and looked into her eyes. They stood there like that, not speaking, for several moments. Then Manoah looked up to heaven.

"Lord," he prayed, "please, I ask You, let this man that You sent to my wife come back to us. Let him tell

Samson

us what we are to do with the boy when he is born—how we are to raise him and what we are to do."

The next day Manoah was again working in the field. Today his wife was in the field, too, but she was not working. She was just sitting, her head bowed, thinking of the day before. Suddenly she sensed she was not alone. She looked up.... There he was, the same tall, straight figure, the same face like polished bronze, the same wonderful eyes.

Once again she ran to her husband. And as yesterday, he looked up when he saw her coming.

"Husband!" she said. "He is back! The man who came to me yesterday has returned. He is over there, not far from here."

Manoah took his wife's hand and went with her. The man was still there, where Manoah's wife had been sitting. Manoah came up to him slowly and stopped before he was too close. Suddenly he felt it would not be wise to stand too close to this man before him. And he, too, like his wife the day before, felt his hands and his knees trembling.

"Sir," Manoah said, "are you—please tell me—are you the man who talked with my wife yesterday?"

"I am," the man said.

"So then, as you have spoken, may it come to pass! Tell me, please, sir, how we are to raise the boy? What

Samson

are we to do with him?"

"Your wife must do everything I told her to do. She must not eat anything that comes of the vine, or drink any wine, or other strong drink, or eat any of the forbidden foods."

Then the stranger turned as if to depart. Manoah held up his hands. "Please!" Manoah said. "Do not leave us yet! Please stay with us a little and let me serve you. I will go and bring a young goat and cook it for you."

"If I do stay, I will not eat your food. But if you wish to prepare it, burn it as an offering to the Lord."

"Tell us your name," said Manoah, "so that we can honor you when your words come true."

"Why do you ask me my name? It is a name full of wonder."

Manoah did not dare say anything more. He ran to his little flock and brought a young goat back to the field where the stranger was still standing. There was a large rock nearby. Manoah cut up the goat and placed the pieces on the rock. Then he laid some sheaves of wheat on the rock and set fire to them.

The flames greedily devoured the dry sheaves, and then the smoke began rising thick and oily as the fire ate into the carcass of the goat.

Then as Manoah and his wife watched, the man walked up to the rock and pointed at the fire with his right hand. Suddenly the fire erupted into a single, solid sheet of white-blue flame, and just as suddenly the crackling and hissing were gone, as if a door had shut out all sound.

Manoah and his wife just stared. Then, as one, they gasped. The man stepped into the middle of the blue flame!

And suddenly that flame shot up into the sky, up and up and up, into the clouds. And the man in the flame, his robe as bright as the sun at midday, rose up with that flame until he was out of sight.

"So he *was* an angel of God!" Manoah said. And he and his wife bowed down to the ground, trembling. "Now we are going to die!" said Manoah, "because we have seen God!"

Manoah's wife said, her voice weak and shaking, "Surely, if the Lord had meant to kill us, He would not have accepted this, our offering. Nor would He have told us all the things He did, or shown us all these things."

They remained like this, faces to the ground, for several minutes. When they got up, the fire, and everything that was on the rock, was gone. The rock was clean, almost dazzling, like fine, bleached linen.

Samson

Manoah's wife did obey the word of the Lord. And, as the Lord had told her, she did have a son. She and Manoah named him Samson.

They lived in a place called "Mahaneh Dan," the "Camp of Dan." Dan was the tribe Manoah belonged to. This place, this "camp," was in the hill country to the east of the Valley of Sorek. Here the boy Samson grew. And, true to the Lord's command, Manoah and his wife did not cut their son's hair. And as he grew, so grew his hair. As his hair grew, so did his strength.

Secret Code:

_____ _____ _____ _____
2-2-6-2   5-1-2-1   1-1-1-1   7-2-9-1

_____ _____ _____
6-2-1-1   8-1-1-2   1-3-3-3

_____ _____ _____ _____,
3-1-8-2   2-2-1-1   3-1-2-3   5-3-1-7

_____ _____ _____
6-5-4-1   1-2-3-2   3-3-6-5

3
The Nazirite Vow

It was past the midday, in the time of the harvest. A boy of about twelve was picking grapes with his father in the vineyard. The man worked steadily, smoothly. There was a simple elegance in the way his hands reached through the tangles of leaves and came out again, without pause or effort, clutching bunches of grapes and laying them neatly in the basket on the path at the man's feet. His face, though weathered by many years of hot summer sun and harsh winter winds, showed no strain or care. And his eyes were kind. He shuffled slowly along the path, his hands working as if they had a mind and will of their own.

The boy was tall and thin, with hands and feet that seemed too big for the rest of his body. Except for one thing he would have appeared like any other boy of his age. His hair looked more like a girl's than a boy's. Black and shimmering like a raven, it was tied back from the boy's face and lay like a thick black rope along his back.

But in every other respect, he was indeed a boy. While his father worked steadily on, his hands never stopping, the boy did not remain in one spot for more than a minute. He would reach into the vines and, with his arms buried almost to the shoulders in leaves and his mouth twisted in a grimace of effort, the vines would rustle and crackle as the boy's hands thrashed among them. Then, *snap!* The vine would shudder and recoil from the violent tug of the boy's large, clumsy hands, which then would emerge in triumph from the leaves, clutching half-crushed, dripping clusters of grapes. These the boy would throw with a *splat* into the basket. Then, fresh from this newest victory, the boy would dart down the path to grab a stick and send it whirring over the rows of vines, or he would suddenly pick up a stone from the path and stalk, in a deep crouch like a tiger, a blackbird that had just landed on the path ahead.

His kindhearted father had learned not to worry about these would-be victims of the boy's. The boy never came close. But the father had noticed, indeed, that though the boy's aim was poor, his power was a marvel. The stone would disappear into the sky— anywhere in the sky—with an angry, throbbing hum.

All through the day the boy would wipe his

stained hands on his tunic and pants. At evening, when his father would load the last basket of grapes on the cart and then turn down the path for home, the boy's chest and legs would be smeared a deep red. His face, too, for he would eat of the grapes during the day and wipe his mouth with the backs of his hands.

On one of these nights, not long ago, the boy's mother stood in the doorway of their house and watched father and son returning from the vineyards. There was her boy, as he was every night, swinging along easily, his hands gesturing with energy, his boyish voice eager, his tunic and pants smeared, as always, in. . . This night her breath caught with a little gasp. *A warrior returning from battle!* His hands and clothes smeared in blood. Her heart faltered for a moment. No, she had not forgotten. She had never forgotten. But. . .he was still a boy. Just a boy.

"Father," the boy said today, "tell me again. What is a Nazirite?"

His father straightened up and looked at the boy. *How he has grown!* the father thought. Was it that long ago that. . . ? It seemed like only the other day.

The man and his wife had told the boy, not too many years ago, the story of his birth. They had told him of the angel of God who had appeared to them and told them about the boy who was to be born to them. They had told the boy of the things the angel said to his mother. But they had not told him everything. Not quite everything. Not yet. . .

But this question was one of the boy's favorites. And the father, who was called Manoah, was always pleased to tell him as often as the boy asked. Manoah had long ago memorized this part in the Law of Moses. He could tell it now, word for word as it was written, though he often liked to put it in his own words.

"The Lord God gave our father Moses this command," began Manoah. "When any man or woman shall make a special vow, the vow of a Nazirite, to dedicate himself to the Lord, he, or she, must not drink any wine or other strong drink. He must not eat or drink anything that is made from grapes, not dried, nor moist, nor even the seeds or the husk. As long as he—"

"But Father, was I not—am I not. . . ?"

"A Nazirite?"

The boy nodded.

His father smiled. He looked at the boy's eager face, smeared with the grapes he had been eating all day. "According to the word of the angel who spoke to your mother and me, yes, you are, my son," Manoah said.

Samson

"Then why. . . ?" The boy stared at his stained hands.

"I do not know why the angel said what he did, my son," Manoah said. "To me, God is a mystery. But the angel told your mother that *she* was not to eat or drink anything from the vine or any of the forbidden foods. For you, the angel said only that we were never to cut your hair. That is all he said of you. And this we have obeyed. To God, I think, that is enough—that we obey."

"But, then, what of the other things?"

"Yes, the other things. As long as a Nazirite is under the vow, he must not cut his hair or shave his beard. His hair is the sign of his dedication to God. . . ."

"So then, that is *my* sign!" said the boy. "I am dedicated to God, am I not?"

"You are," said his father.

"But go on, please. Tell me the rest."

Manoah smiled again. "A Nazirite must also never defile himself by going near a corpse, not even of his father, mother, sister, or brother. As long as he is a Nazirite, he is dedicated to the Lord. But when the time of his dedication is over, then he may shave his beard and cut his hair, and he may drink wine."

"What is the time of a Nazirite's dedication?"

"The time that he himself has chosen, the time he has vowed to dedicate himself to the Lord and to the Lord's service."

"But I—what is my time, then?"

Manoah looked steadily at his son's face for several moments. "Ah," the man said, "your time, I think, is chosen by the Lord Himself. That is the mystery. You did not choose this course for your life, nor did we, your mother and father. The Lord God has decided the time of your dedication for you, my son. What time He has chosen, only He knows. It may be for the whole time that you are upon this earth."

And Manoah, staring now out over the vineyards, said to himself, *I think perhaps it will be for the whole time that he is upon this earth. And I hope. . .I hope it will be a long time. . . .*

That night Manoah sat at the table mending a basket. The boy's mother was baking bread. The boy was sitting on the floor, carving a long piece of wood.

"Samson," the boy's mother said. The boy looked up. "What is that you are carving?" she asked.

"A sword," he said.

She looked sharply at her husband, who caught her eye.

"I am making a sword to fight the Philistines,"

Samson

Samson said. He heard his mother's little gasp. He looked at her. There was something in her face, some look, that he had never seen before. "Not really," he said. "I am pretending."

"I...I thought you were through pretending," his mother said. She tried to smile. "You are so grown!"

"When I *am* grown," Samson said, "I want to be a warrior." He scrambled to his feet and swung his wooden sword. "I want to strike the Philistines."

"There are no warriors among our people anymore," his father said. "Only shepherds and vinedressers."

"And slaves!" Samson said.

"The people of Israel are *not* slaves!" his father said. "We are the children of the living God."

"But why do the Philistines treat us like slaves, then?"

"Because they are an evil people."

"But if we are the children of God, why does He not protect us; why does He not fight our enemies for us?"

Manoah sighed. "Ah," he said, "He would if only ...He does, whenever we...Israel does not remember her God. We have done evil again and again. We worship other gods, and we do not obey our own God. And the Lord God warns us again and again, but we do not listen. And so, for a time, we...we are—"

"Slaves!" said Samson.

Manoah said nothing. He worked steadily, quietly on his basket. Samson sat down again and continued carving his stick. After a while he looked up.

"Father," he said, "we have always obeyed God, haven't we?"

"Aye," said Manoah. "And so we shall, always."

"Then perhaps God will deliver *us*, at least, from the Philistines."

Manoah looked at his son and smiled. "The important thing is to obey God," Manoah said. "That we can always do, no matter if we are slaves or free. Only God knows what will be. Our part is just to love Him and obey Him."

Samson looked down at his piece of wood. He stared at his hands, wrapped around his "sword." Somehow they seemed just now like hands that were not his own. They were so big. And so ugly. Whose hands were they, if they were not his own?

The smell of baking bread filled the room. The

Samson

fire in the pit cast a mellow hue over the stone hearth. Samson's mother picked up the tunic he had worn in the vineyards that day and held it up in the firelight. She shook her head and smiled. "As long as you return from the fields like this, my son, I will know that you are not yet grown."

Her husband, watching her, noticed that her hands, as they held out the boy's shirt, were trembling.

Secret Code:

$\overline{}$ $\overline{}$ $\overline{}$ $\overline{}$,
3-1-4-4 1-2-8-2 5-1-7-2 4-3-3-3

$\overline{}$ $\overline{}$ $\overline{}$ $\overline{}$ $\overline{}$
2-3-7-2 1-2-4-4 7-2-4-3 6-1-7-5 8-2-2-4

$\overline{}$ $\overline{}$ $\overline{}$,
9-1-3-8 1-1-9-1 5-8-2-6

4
Lion Slayer

The door to the cottage burst open. The old man and his wife looked up, startled.

"Oh, it is you," the man said. "Please, Samson, do not frighten your poor old mother and father so."

"I am sorry, Father," said the young man who strode into the room. He gave the

door a careless little push, and it slammed shut with a rattle.

Samson had grown. His hands, though even larger than ever, were no longer too big for the rest of him. He was tall, so tall he had to stoop a little to come in through the doorway to this place, the house of his parents and the home of his boyhood. And his hair, black as pitch, was now tied in seven long locks that hung down his back.

"Please forgive me, Mother, Father. I did not mean to frighten you." But now his face lit up with a grin. "I have been to Timnah," he said.

"Yes, I know," said his father. "I sent you there, remember? To buy some—"

"Oh, yes. Some—I am sorry, I forgot. But, Father! I have had such a happy distraction. While I was there I saw a girl. And. . ." He sat down now at the table with his mother and father. "And I—she is the girl I want to marry!"

"In Timnah!" said his father. He looked at his wife, who caught his eye. "That is a city of the Philistines. Is this girl. . .is she. . . ?"

"She is—yes—a Philistine. But—"

"A Philistine?" said his father. "Can you not find a girl among our own people, son? Surely there is someone here that you—"

"I have never seen anyone like her, Father."

"But, Samson, you are an Israelite. A Danite. You know the laws of our people. It is forbidden for us to marry among the heathen."

"But is this a sin? Perhaps she does not worship other gods. Perhaps she may even choose to worship the God of Israel."

Samson

His father did not answer.

"Does God care, even?" said Samson. "Has He not abandoned us to live like slaves? Does He care so much about a thing such as marriage? Love and marriage among the slaves!"

His father looked sharply at him. "Do not tempt the Lord, my son!"

Samson looked down. "I am sorry," he said. "I. . .I did not mean to speak of the Lord so." He looked up again. "But, Father"—and Samson looked pleadingly at his mother, too—"does God not care about love? I wish to marry the woman I love."

His mother said, rather weakly, "Samson, how do you know that you cannot find a girl among our own people that you can love?"

Samson pushed his chair back and stood up. "I only know that this girl is the one I want to marry." He looked at his father. "Will you get her for me?"

Again his father did not answer.

"If you will not get her for me, will you at least give me your blessing?" Samson said.

"We will go with you to Timnah," his father said. "And we will see."

Samson's mother and father did not know, but it

Samson

was the Lord Himself who was leading Samson to do this. The time had come. Samson's work was about to begin.

Timnah was only a morning's walk from the Camp of Dan. Near Timnah the road passed through wide-spreading vineyards. Samson was walking alone. He had gone ahead of his mother and father, who planned to follow him later in the day.

Just then he heard something, off somewhere in the vineyard. It was a noise he had heard before, and he knew at once what it was. A lion.

Samson stopped. He had heard lions before, but not often, and never very close. His father had taught him to be very quiet whenever he heard a lion, and to crouch down low, so his scent would not be carried by the breezes over the rows of vines to the lion. He had done this from time to time as a boy. Each time, the feeling that came over him was exactly the same. There was a deep sense of awe mixed with terror, a powerful sense of the presence of something at once terrible and majestic—and a feeling of utter helplessness. As a boy, having never seen a lion before, Samson knew, the very first time he heard one—somehow he just *knew*—that the thick, wiry rows of vines would be no more protection than a spider's web if the lion only knew he was there.

This lion was close, closer than Samson had ever

heard one before. And it was a mighty roar. A young lion, by the sound. Strangely, Samson felt none of his old dread just now. For a moment he was puzzled. What *did* he feel? He clenched his teeth. His hands were knotted in fists. What was this hot emotion suddenly surging through his breast?

Anger. Pure, white-hot anger.

The lion roared again, this time closer. Samson did not know why he did what he did just then. He did not wonder about it. He did not think about it all. He just did it.

He reared his head back, and he roared. His voice bellowed out across the vineyard, as loud as, and perhaps even more frightening than, the lion's.

And there was something else Samson did not know just then. He would come to understand something of it later, but not now. This was the first time in his life that it happened. But it would not be the last. The power of the Lord had come over him.

The roar of the lion came again, much closer, just a few rows away. Samson turned off the road, into the vineyard. He strutted down the path, slapping at the leaves on the vines, kicking stones in the path. Cower and hide? Not this time! "Come on, lion!" he shouted.

And it came. There was a tremendous crackling and snapping through the rows of vines, just yards ahead, another ear-splitting roar, and the lion was in Samson's path.

Samson had been right in his guess. It was a young lion, its mane not yet long and thick. But it was nearly full-grown, its body tall and thin. It fixed its cold yellow eyes on Samson now, and it charged, a tawny blur of snarling rage.

Samson did not even have time to crouch, to brace himself. But as quick as the lion was, Samson's hands were quicker. They came together like a steel trap on the lion's throat just as the lion sprang. The lion's victory roar was cut off suddenly with a choking gurgle. And those hands, those great hands clutched and tore and pulled and ripped. Samson's eyes flashed like fire; his white teeth were clenched in fury.

And then it was over. The lion hung limp in Samson's grasp. Samson threw the bloody, torn carcass from him, and it struck the dusty earth with a great thud, its limbs flopping awkwardly.

Samson stood there glaring in hatred at his victim,

his hands still clenched, his chest heaving.

And then like a violent summer storm that comes up suddenly and almost as suddenly passes, Samson's passion was gone. His hands hung loose at his sides. He was not panting now, though his breath came and went with a shuddering tremor. He looked down at his hands. They were covered in blood. Lion's blood!

And suddenly it came to Samson. He had killed a lion with his bare hands!

He was shaking all over now. He turned to go down the path. His legs felt weak. As he walked slowly back to the road, he heard a voice, a voice from his memory. It was his father's voice.

"You did not choose this course for your life. . . .
The Lord God Himself has decided the time of your dedication for you, my son. . . . What time He has chosen, only He knows. . . ."

Samson

Secret Code:

_____ _____ _____ _____ _____ _____ _____ _____
1-1-2-4   2-3-2-2   5-2-6-3   7-3-1-2   6-2-1-3   1-1-6-1   3-1-2-5   4-1-5-3

_____ _____, _____
1-4-1-3   6-1-3-4   7-2-3-1

_____ _____ _____ _____
6-4-9-4   2-1-2-3   3-3-4-3   1-2-4-1

_____ _____ _____ _____,
4-1-1-1   6-2-4-4   7-3-5-3   1-1-1-3

5
The Riddle

Samson had not told anyone about the lion that day, not even his mother and father. He had gone on to Timnah, to the girl's house. He had talked with the girl and her father. The girl had agreed to marry Samson, and her father gave them his blessing. Then Samson had gone home again with his parents. He would return for the girl, he promised her. They would be married there, in her father's house.

Today was the day for Samson's wedding celebration to begin. He went this time with his mother and father. The road was now passing through the vineyards before Timnah.

Samson stopped. He was looking off into the vineyard to the right side of the road.

"Is something wrong, Samson?" his father asked.

Samson

"No, I. . . You two go on ahead. I will catch up to you in a moment."

His mother and father were watching him, a question written on their faces.

"Please, do," Samson said. "I will just be a moment. I want to see something."

He waited until they had turned and started walking; then he plunged in through the rows of vines. *It was near here,* he thought. *This must be the place.* He just wanted to see. . . . Yes, this was it. Which row? They all looked the same. *The next one,* he thought. He stepped through a little gap in the hedge.

There it was! His heart was beating hard now. He walked slowly toward the thing on the path just ahead, then stood there staring down at it.

Samson's brow was suddenly creased. Oh, what a disappointment! His fearsome enemy, whom he had met in deadly combat and destroyed, was only a shrunken, distorted bag of skin! The lion's insides were gone, dried out or, more likely, devoured by scavengers. Blackish leathery flesh clung to bleached white ribs.

Victory had been sweet—oh, so sweet. *But in the end,* Samson thought now, *death—any death—is only. . . ugly.*

But now what was this? A humming sound was coming from. . .from inside the lion's carcass. Samson knelt down to look inside the hollow chest under the ribs. Bees. And honey! A honeycomb the size of a melon was clinging to the lion's rib cage. Samson reached in quickly, grabbed and pulled, and then jumped to his feet and ran, before the bees could defend their home.

Samson came out into the road now, the spoil of his victory, a great mass of golden, dripping deliciousness, cupped in his hands. He ate some as he walked. Soon he caught up to his mother and father. His mother stared in surprise at the thing in Samson's hands.

"I. . .I was right, you see," he said. "I thought I had smelled honey. It was not far from the path." He held out his treasure. "Here, have some!"

In Timnah there was a feast today. This was the first of seven days of celebrating, of wine and roasts and pastries and songs and dancing. On the seventh and last day of this festival there would be a wedding. This was the custom among the people of Timnah.

It was also the custom for the bridegroom to have his friends celebrate with him. But Samson did not have friends here. These were not his people. They were Philistines.

"But you *will* have friends here," the father of the

bride told Samson. "Thirty companions for the bridegroom. That is our way." And so he had invited these "companions" to join Samson in the feasting and celebrating. And these young men came gladly. So what if this tall stranger with the long black locks was not of their own people—they were only too pleased to help themselves to seven days of feasting.

On the second day of the feast Samson was sitting with his thirty "friends." They had all had much wine.

"Friends," Samson said. "Let me tell you a riddle. And I offer you a wager. If you can tell me the answer to my riddle before the seven days of our feast are up, I will give each one of you a new shirt and cloak."

Faces turned to him in interest and curiosity.

"But if you cannot tell me, then you must each give me a new shirt and cloak," Samson continued. "What do you say?"

"Tell us your riddle! We will wager," they said.

"So then, listen. Out of the eater came something to eat. Out of the strong came something sweet. Now tell me if you can. What does this mean?" Samson was grinning.

The men looked at one another, embarrassed and puzzled. And they began murmuring and arguing among themselves.

Three days later they still had not one idea among them what this stranger's riddle could mean. And they said to themselves, "Look, what is this foreigner, this Israelite, to us? What do we care about him? Must we allow him to shame us like this?"

And one of them said, "What about his bride-to-be? Suppose he has told her the riddle. Or if he hasn't, suppose she can make him tell."

The thirty men chose their moment when Samson's bride was by herself. Three of them came up to her and said quietly, "Get your husband to tell you the meaning of his riddle. Entice him, trick him; do it any way you can."

"Why? What. . . ?"

One of them brought his face close to hers and hissed savagely, "Because if you don't, we will set fire to your father's house and burn you with it!"

Her breath caught in her throat. These men were serious. Their eyes burned into hers. Then suddenly they turned, smiling and laughing as if they had been sharing a joke with the bride, and rejoined their companions.

She was terrified. What could she do? Her father's house. . . Their lives. . . She looked at Samson on the other side of the room. What would the cost be? Thirty changes of garments in exchange for their lives. Should she tell him? But he was a stranger here, not among friends. What could he do? Her heart was very bitter.

"What is wrong?" Samson asked her when they were alone together. "Your face... What is troubling you?"

For just a moment she thought she would tell him. But then her courage failed her. "You do not love me," she said, burying her face in her hands.

"What! What do you mean?"

"You...you told my friends a riddle and did not even tell me what it means."

"But I have not even told my mother and father! Why should I tell you?"

"You would if you loved me." And she burst into tears.

And for the rest of that day, whenever she could, Samson's bride begged him with tears to tell her. Finally he gave in and, alone in a corner of the room, he whispered the secret of his riddle to her.

On the last day of the feast the bride's father stood up and announced that the moment had come. The wedding ceremony would begin in a moment, he said. And Samson and his daughter would be man and wife.

There were cheers and shouts and clapping. When the noise had died away, one of the thirty companions stood up and held up his hand for silence. He looked at Samson and sneered.

"Tell us a riddle," he said. "What could be sweeter than honey? And what could be stronger than a lion?"

Then the thirty broke out into laughter and jeers. Samson's teeth flashed. He stood up slowly and drew his shoulders back. And suddenly the laughter was gone.

Every one of those thirty men, indeed, everyone in that room, was aware, suddenly and without any doubt, that the man standing there was *dangerous*.

No one spoke a word. All eyes were on the tall man from the Camp of Dan with the long locks down his back.

Then Samson said, through clenched teeth, "If you hadn't been plowing with my heifer, you would not know the answer now."

And without another word he turned and strode out the door.

About a week later Samson was in Timnah again. He walked down the street with a huge armful of brightly colored clothes tied into a bundle with rope.

"Here, you!" he said to a man walking ahead of him. The man turned, startled. Samson had recognized him. He was one of the thirty.

Samson dropped the bundle at the man's feet. "Tell your friends, my *companions*!"—and his teeth ground together as he said this—"that you are all now paid in full!"

Then Samson returned the way he had come.

The man standing in the street with the bundle of clothes at his feet now had even more reason to fear—and hate—this Israelite with the long hair. News had come from Ashkelon, another Philistine city about a day's journey from Timnah, that just a few days ago the bodies of some thirty men of that city were found here and there throughout the city. The men had been beaten and stripped. But, strangely, they had been stripped only of their shirts and cloaks.

Some time after this, during the wheat harvest, Samson went again to Timnah. He wanted to visit his wife. He brought a young goat with him for an offering, as was the custom.

Her father answered the knock at the door. "You!" he said. "I—we did not think we would see you here again."

"I left in. . .in haste, I know," said Samson. "But I

did not intend to stay away. Please accept this, my offering. I wish to conclude our wedding and to visit my wife."

The girl's father suddenly looked a little pale. "I—when you left so suddenly, I thought you had changed your mind about my daughter. I really thought you hated her."

Samson looked sharply at the man. "What are you saying?" he asked.

"I—I—you know, it is the custom. . . . You had left. You left your bride before. . .before the marriage was completed, you know."

Samson's voice was like flint. "What are you *saying*?"

"I had to. . .it is the custom. To save my daughter from disgrace—a terrible thing. I gave her as wife to the best man of the bridegroom's."

Samson's face hardened.

"She is another man's wife," the girl's father said. "But. . .but she has a younger sister, who is prettier. Take her, if you like."

Samson just stood there for several moments, his chest heaving. And his hands slowly curled themselves into knotted fists.

Then he said, as he was turning to go, "This time I

Samson

will be more blameless than the Philistines, for what I do to them!"

Secret Code:

$\overline{}$ $\overline{}$ $\overline{}$
10-1-3-2 1-1-1-6 3-1-6-4

$\overline{}$ $\overline{}$ $\overline{}$ $\overline{}$ $\overline{}$ $\overline{}$-
2-4-8-1 7-2-1-1 6-1-3-2 8-3-1-3 9-2-1-6 2-1-5-1

$\overline{}$ $\overline{}$ $\overline{}$ $\overline{}$ $\overline{}$ $\overline{}$,
3-3-2-1 4-6-2-2 5-1-4-3 6-8-1-2   7-5-2-3 1-2-3-3

6
Fire and Foxes

The wheat was in harvest in the lands of the Philistines. The plains were awash in deep amber waves. Already the harvesters had cut wide swaths through many of the fields, and the sheaves wrapped in twine stood like golden-haired sentinels throughout these great bare stretches. The olives, too, were ripe in the orchards that shared these lands with the wheat.

Tonight a small band of harvest workers were sitting together out in the wheat fields. These were men from Timnah, just beyond the vineyards a little to the east. They had worked until dusk today and would sleep among the sheaves tonight. They were seated in a small circle, talking in hushed voices.

"A fine way to pay a debt, wouldn't you say?" said one.

"What does it matter?" said another. "What are they of Ashkelon to us?"

"They wear nice clothes there, anyway. 'Tis the finest shirt and cloak *I've* ever had."

There was laughter. But one or two of the men did not laugh. "But what if it is true?" said one of these. "What if that Israelite dog did do it?"

"Aye, and we thought to make a fool of him! What if any of us is seen wearing these dead men's clothes?"

No one laughed now. Then one of them said sharply, "Listen! What's that noise?"

They were all silent for a few moments. "Foxes," said one.

"Oh, there are lots of them out here—swarms of them, like flies."

They listened again. Then the men looked at one another in curiosity and, perhaps, in alarm. "I've never heard so many," said one. He stood up and peered out into the darkness. "They're...they're all over!"

The others, too, stood up now. Something was wrong, they knew.

From out of the night came a horrible wailing and screaming, a yelping and screeching. It came from all around them.

"Look!" shouted one of the men.

"Fire!" cried another, pointing.

It was. Everywhere the men looked, the flames were racing across the fields of standing wheat, and as the sheaves caught fire they flared up into the black sky like giant torches.

The men stood in a circle, their backs to one another, and stared in wide-eyed terror. And suddenly they were all staring at something else.

A spot of fire had detached itself from the flaming field in the distance and, as if this little bundle of sparks had a will of its own, came racing across the bare, cropped field toward the men.

It was indeed alive! It cut a ragged, frantic path across the field, running in little circles, crossing its own track and doubling back again. It even had a voice! As it came, it piped and squealed in fear. And behind it, following this erratic path, the flames were already licking and spreading.

Then it was past the men, and they saw what it was: a pair of foxes, their tails tied to a flaming brand that bumped and trailed along, showering sparks.

The men stared at one another for just a moment. Then they all turned and ran for their lives.

By morning all the wheat fields, vineyards, and olive groves of the Philistines were black and bare and smoldering. And the news was going around. Someone had done this. The foxes' tails had been tied together in pairs, the torches lit, and the frenzied, racing animals set loose in the fields. It was cunning work, deliberate and hateful. And the destruction was complete. There was nothing left.

Who? And why? Was it a grudge? A prank? An act of war? But who would dare strike at the Philistines this way?

In Timnah today, thirty men had gathered in an empty street behind a large tavern. They were all speaking in harsh, loud whispers.

"It's that Israelite with the long hair."

"He is the one who killed those men in Ashkelon."

"How do you know?"

"The girl's father. He gave her to the best man."

"But he—the Israelite had left her. He didn't want—"

"No, he did. He returned to her father's house for her, and he was refused."

"How do you know?"

"I saw him! He gave me the shirts and cloaks in the street and told me to give them to the rest of you. I followed him—don't worry, he didn't see me—to the girl's house."

"So, then, what is this? Revenge? Against us? Why burn the fields outside the city?"

"Because, fool, they are *our* fields! The Philistines. He is an Israelite."

"Then he is the fool! Does he think he can get away with this?"

"He will pay!"

"Aye, we will make him pay!"

There was nothing anyone could do now. The house was engulfed in flames. The people stood in the street in grim silence, watching. No one had come out of the house. There had been screams from inside just moments ago. But then they were gone, and the fire just raged now, through the windows and out of the crackling timbers of the roof.

A tall, black-haired man was pushing his way through the crowd. "No!" he cried in an anguished voice. He ran to the doorway of the house but then staggered backward, his hands over his eyes. The open doorway was a sheet of blue-orange flame.

"Come back!" came shouts from the crowd.

"There is nothing you can do!"

The man turned to the crowd. "Did. . .did anyone escape?" He gasped.

Several of the people shook their heads.

Samson

"No one? No one!" The man's voice rose to an agonized shriek. "No one at all? Oh, God, my God, was there no one—?" Suddenly his face changed. His eyes were fixed on a lone man at the edge of the crowd.

"You!" The voice was like a clap of thunder. "You were one of them! Where are your—? You! And you, and you, and you! So you are all here! Friends! My friends! The friends of the bridegroom!"

"With a wedding present for you!" said one of the thirty or so men who were now clustered together. Several of them had clubs in their hands.

"A present for Samson," one said. "A pretty present for the pretty man with a woman's hair!"

There was cruel, mocking laughter.

The crowd watching this scene began fading back into the darkness of the street.

The man was alone with his enemies. He stood still as though carved in stone. His eyes were like ice. Just now this man, with a woman's hair and a giant's hands, was not pretty.

To many in the crowd watching from the shadows now, he looked like Death.

And then Death moved. With a single leap he sprang on the nearest man. Before the man could raise his club, Samson had wrenched it out of his hand and brought it down like a giant's hammer on the man's skull.

Samson was among them now like a reaper with a

scythe among the wheat. They fell quickly, like stalks of corn, one after another after another.

In the space of several heartbeats, fewer than a dozen men were still standing. They ran off now screaming, leaving their clubs lying in the street.

The rest of the crowd, too, began scattering everywhere. They had seen enough.

That night in the city of Timnah the call was going around: Their enemy had visited them tonight. A titan—a man of great power—had come among men. The Reaper had laid his grim hand upon them.

And word spread quickly. This was the same Reaper that had swept through Ashkelon not too long ago. The same who had burned all the wheat and all the vineyards and all the olives just days ago.

But this enemy was, after all, only a man, and the man had a name: Samson! Of the Israelites!

The men of Timnah were gathering tonight. If this man Samson wished for enemies, he had them now!

Samson

Secret Code:

$\overline{\rule{0.8cm}{0pt}}$ $\overline{\rule{0.8cm}{0pt}}$ $\overline{\rule{0.8cm}{0pt}}$ $\overline{\rule{0.8cm}{0pt}}$ $\overline{\rule{0.8cm}{0pt}}$
2-2-3-2 5-3-3-1 4-1-7-2 1-3-1-1 6-2-1-1

$\overline{\rule{0.8cm}{0pt}}$ $\overline{\rule{0.8cm}{0pt}}$ $\overline{\rule{0.8cm}{0pt}}$ $\overline{\rule{0.8cm}{0pt}}$,
7-3-5-3 1-1-1-2 2-1-4-5 6-5-3-4

$\overline{\rule{0.8cm}{0pt}}$ $\overline{\rule{0.8cm}{0pt}}$ $\overline{\rule{0.8cm}{0pt}}$ $\overline{\rule{0.8cm}{0pt}}$
7-4-2-2 6-4-2-6 2-3-3-1 3-6-7-5

7
The Donkey's Jawbone

There was alarming news in the town of Lehi today. An army of Philistines was camped on the plain not far away. This was the land of the tribe of Judah, the people of Samson's mother.

Word spread quickly throughout Lehi. All the men of Judah who lived here, all the men able to go to war, were gathering together. They chose a captain to lead them. But they had no desire for war. There were at least a few thousand Philistines here—soldiers with armored breastplates and helmets, with spears and swords, and with iron chariots. The men of Judah had not even a single sword for every man. Most of these men were shepherds and farmers. At the call to gather for battle, they had grabbed any weapons they could, even anything they might use for weapons—wooden staves, picks, axes. The Judahites had few metal tools, and fewer weapons still.

The Judahites were all agreed that they must avoid war with this Philistine army. The captain chose a handful of men to go with him to talk with the Philistines.

The captain of the Philistines came out to meet them.

"Why have you come to attack us?" the Judahite captain asked. "What have we done to you?"

The Philistine captain said, "You are hiding a murderer."

The men of Judah looked at one another in alarm.

"His name is Samson," the Philistine captain continued. "He is our enemy. We have been told that his home is near here. He is hiding from us, somewhere near here. We have come to take him prisoner and to do to him what he has done to us!"

"But this man, Samson, is not one of us," the Judahite captain said. "We do not know him. If he is hiding among us, he has hidden himself from us as well."

"We will have Samson, or we will have all of you! Turn him over to us or we will attack. You have until the setting of the sun this day!"

Samson

When the Judahite captain and his men returned to town, they asked the rest of the men about Samson. Of course the name Samson was already well-known in the land of Judah. It had been told how he had burned the wheat and vineyards and olives of the Philistines. And there were rumors that he had killed many of the Philistines, too. But no one dared speak of this openly.

Now, though, several of the men here spoke up. "We know where he is hiding," they said. They pointed to the cliffs in the east. "In Etam, in a cave."

"We have until the evening today to turn him over to the Philistines," the captain said. "If we do not, we will be destroyed."

"But this man, Samson, he's one of us!" said one.

"He does not live among us."

"He is of Judah! Does that count for nothing?"

"Would you have all of us die for one man?" This one swept his arm out toward the town. "The Philistines will kill everyone, you know! Every man, woman, and child. And we can do nothing to stop them."

The captain held up his hand. "Let's go to Samson," he said. "We must speak with him, at least."

"Sir," said one, "it is said, you know, that this man is a Nazirite. It is said that the power of God makes him strong." Several of the men nodded grimly. "It is said, even, that he has been chosen by the Lord to deliver our people from the Philistines."

"Aye," said another. "So it is said! Do we wish to go

against the anointed of God, if this is true?"

"It *is* true!" said still another. "He slaughtered scores of Philistines alone and with his bare hands, in their very own streets! Even if he were not anointed by God, sent for our deliverance, he is still a dangerous foe! It would not be well to have this man for an enemy!"

"Would you rather have him as an enemy, or the entire Philistine army out there?" This one gestured toward the plain.

The captain spoke again. "Men of Judah, we must make a choice! This one man or our wives, our children, our homes. And who knows? It may be that the Philistines will not kill him. We will go together, all of us. There are some three thousand of us. I think," he said with a mocking grin, "that should be enough against one man."

Samson saw them coming. He came down from the cave to meet them.

"What have you done to us?" the captain said to him. "Do you not know that the Philistines are our rulers?"

"I have done to the Philistines only as they did to me," Samson said.

Samson

"They can do with us as they please. You have brought them down upon us!"

"What have you come to do with me?" Samson asked.

"We must turn you over to the Philistines," the captain said. "We have come to bind you with rope and deliver you to them."

Was that a smile that just crossed Samson's face? The men standing nearest to him began backing away nervously.

But Samson said, "Give me your word that you will not kill me yourselves."

"We give you our word. We will only bind you with rope."

"All right, bind me." He held out his arms.

It was a new rope, thick as a man's wrist. They bound Samson's arms and coiled the rope around and around him, leaving only his legs free. They brought him this way to the camp of the Philistines.

And now a cry went throughout the Philistine camp. "Samson!" And the Philistines rushed out toward Samson, shouting and laughing. The Judahites turned and fled.

The Philistines were closing in on Samson. He stood calmly without blinking. . .waiting.

And then, as he knew it would, it happened. He felt it surge through him, just as he had felt it that first time, that day he had faced the lion. The power of God was upon him.

Samson took a deep, deep breath and—*snap!* He burst through the rope as if it were a burnt thread. The Philistines nearest him stopped suddenly, just as they were reaching out to grab him.

Then Samson spotted something on the ground at his feet. It was white and curved, like a... It was a jawbone. He grabbed it. A donkey's jawbone, not dry and brittle, but fresh, with a good heft to it.

The Philistines had surrounded Samson. The cries came from all around, "Kill him! Destroy him!" But the faces of those nearest to Samson were wary. He had just snapped his ropes like a child breaking a blade of grass. The rest of the army, though, had not seen this. They surged toward Samson, pressing those in front closer and closer to him.

Then Samson himself attacked. The jawbone in his hand whistled and sang through the air. Its voice was a shriek of terror to the Philistines, the voice of death. The Philistines leaped at Samson in a frenzy and swung their swords in fury—but one by one they crumpled and lay on the ground.

More and more they poured in, screaming and

crazed by hatred and terror. Samson swung and swung, left and right, pressed back and farther back as the Philistines kept coming, and as their twitching, sprawling bodies piled one on top of another.

Finally the ground was so covered by the bodies of Philistines that the rest of the army had to tread on them to get to Samson—and he piled them yet higher and higher as they came.

Then the frenzy was over. Hatred had forsaken the rest of the Philistines. But fear remained—and conquered. They stood now and just stared at their enemy, his arms covered in blood, standing there like a giant on an island amid a sea of broken and bloodied armor. Then they turned and fled back across the plain.

Samson stood alone, gasping, his chest heaving. The power of God lifted off of him now, like the dew rising in the morning sun, and was gone. His arms and hands, then his knees, began to quiver. The hand still holding the jawbone was shaking, but it would not let go of the jawbone. He took the bone with his other hand and pried it loose with fingers that felt like wood. He threw the bone away and then staggered over and through the bodies that surrounded him.

Samson

Samson stumbled and tripped as he went and finally collapsed at the base of the cliff, near the cave where he had been hiding. His throat was so dry he could barely breathe.

Then, perhaps for the first time in his life, he prayed.

"Lord God," he said, "You have given me victory. With the jawbone of a donkey I have killed"—he looked out over the bodies on the plain, guessing at their number—"a thousand men. I will call this place Ramath Lehi." This meant "the lifting up of the jaw."

Then Samson crawled over to the cliff and sat with his back against the rock. He was very thirsty and weak.

"Lord," he prayed again, "You gave me this victory. Am I now going to die of thirst and be captured by these heathen Philistines?" He leaned his head back against the rock and closed his eyes.

Then he felt something curious, something wet and dripping on his shoulder. He opened his eyes to look.

From a crack in the rock above his head, water was trickling! Samson struggled to his feet. And suddenly it began gushing out over his face, cold and clear. He plunged his head under this little flow and drank with great slurping gulps.

Samson

His thirst was quenched; the weakness was gone. He felt refreshed and strong.

"Thank You, Lord," he said. "You have restored my life. Now I think I will call this place En Hakkore."

And this is what this place has been called ever since—"the well of him that cried."

Secret Code:

_____ _____ _____ _____
1-1-1-1   5-4-2-2   9-1-2-3   8-1-1-1

_____ _____ _____ _____,
2-3-5-2   3-2-1-1   1-2-3-4   7-2-3-3

_____ _____ _____ _____,
8-4-2-5   2-1-5-2   3-5-5-3   4-2-1-5

8
The Power of God

The cities the Philistines controlled in this land ran up along the Mediterranean coast—Gaza, Ashkelon, and Ashdod were nearest the coast, and then Ekron and Gezer were a little farther inland. These cities formed a sort of net for the Philistines, through which anyone traveling to or from the coast had to pass.

The southernmost of these cities was Gaza. This was a city of great strength and importance to the Philistines. It was walled in all around, with gates of thick iron bars. And it was the center of great caravan trading routes that went south to Arabia, south and west to Egypt, south and east to Edom, and north along the Mediterranean coast and overland to Damascus in the land of Syria, and beyond. The people of the Philistines who lived in this city had great wealth from the thriving trade they carried on, both by land and by sea.

But tonight reports were going around the city of something that had become more important to all the people of the Philistines than their riches, their powerful armies, or their great houses and palaces and temples.

Samson! He was here tonight.

That name was hated now among the Philistines in all their land. He was their worst enemy—perhaps, just now, their only enemy.

It was growing dark. A group of about twenty men, Philistines, had gathered in the narrow street. They were arguing, though they did not raise their voices above a loud whisper.

"Here, tonight? He couldn't be."

"But he is! I saw him."

"How could he be such a fool as to walk right into our city alone like that? Does he think he is one of the gods?"

"It is said that he is, you know."

"He is no god!"

"Then how does he possess such great strength? Have you not heard what he did to the army from Timnah? He slaughtered more than a thousand."

"Alone?"

Samson

"Aye, alone! With the jawbone of a donkey!"

"If this is true, what can we do against him?"

"Yes, what can we do? We would be fools to—"

"We would be fools only if we met him in battle. But what if we took him by surprise? We will kill him before he even knows he is in danger."

"If he can be killed, that is."

"Of course he can be killed! Or do you, too, believe that he is a god?"

"I don't know. . . ."

"Look, whoever is not with us, say so now and go your way. The rest of us will be in this together. Think! There is a reward for his capture or death, you know. We will be rich men, all for a short night's work."

"But which house did he go to? No one saw."

"It is near here, one of these."

"We cannot risk breaking into someone's house. We would be hanged as robbers."

"We can wait until morning. Do you not think Samson will wish to steal away from here before the day gets on and people are about?"

"But then what of us? Would it not be better to do this thing under cover of night? He would surely see us and—"

"No, he will not see us! We will wait in hiding. Over there." He pointed to an alley. "We can see all these houses from there, and we cannot be seen ourselves. When he comes out—it must be one of those few houses—we will fall in behind him and take him by surprise. And, look, we are near the gate, too. He cannot pass out that way before we see him."

The night was black. There was no moon tonight. The houses along the street were dark and silent. The assassins waiting in the alley were asleep but for one or two who were keeping watch. Suddenly one of these heard a noise. A very slight noise but unmistakable. Someone had opened a door. The watcher peered across the dark street at the houses. He knew he had heard the creaky hinges of a door. But it was so hard to see anything. Wait, what was that? Yes, someone was moving. The shadowy form was in the street now, moving. . .toward the city gate! The watcher's heart was thumping. He nudged the other watcher, not daring to speak. This one whispered into his ear, "Yes, I see. I cannot see who it is. Can you?"

"No, it is too dark. But it is a man, I am sure. He is tall. Let's wake the others, quietly!"

Samson had awakened just past midnight. Something had wakened him. What? He did not know, but he was wide awake now and

Samson

he sat up in bed. He was troubled. He was among his enemies here, he knew, yet no one could have seen him today, could they? Perhaps. He got dressed and stole down the stairs. As he slowly opened the door the rusted hinges creaked, and he groaned softly. Then he was out in the street and walking quickly toward the city gate.

Samson did not know that an angel of the Lord had wakened him, or that the angel had whispered a warning to him to flee the city. Samson only knew that something was troubling him and that he should get away from here. He believed in God, and he had more than once felt the power of God. He had even prayed once, and the Lord had answered his prayer. But he was not used to praying or to listening to the Lord's voice.

Nor did Samson know just now that twenty Philistines were sneaking up behind him in the street. The gate was just up ahead. The Philistines were closing in, quickly, silently. Knives and swords were drawn.

But the Lord knew. Suddenly Samson felt it happening again. Something welled up in his breast, and he felt that same tingling in his hands that he remembered from before, and they began trembling. The power of God had come over him.

He stopped and reared back his head. The men were just behind him. The few nearest Samson raised their swords to strike in unison. Then Samson roared. It was the roar of a lion, the bellow of a giant. The Philistines dropped their swords and knives from hands that were suddenly paralyzed.

And Samson strode up to the gate, planted his feet solidly, and took hold of the bars with both hands. Power surged through his limbs. His shoulders knotted and bunched and, with another deafening roar, he wrenched with all his might. The iron bars shrieked and groaned, and the massive posts rang out as they snapped loose from their stone moorings.

The group of men watching could not move, could not turn and run. They just stood there, watching what they would have refused to believe if they had not seen it with their own eyes.

Samson heaved the whole city gate and its posts up over his head and behind him, planting them squarely on his shoulders. Then he walked out through the empty gateway and disappeared in the night.

He would carry the gate and posts a long way tonight. A long, long way—tonight, the next day, the night after, and the day after that. He would come, finally, to the top of a hill looking out over the city of Hebron, and there he dumped the gate on the ground.

The gate of Gaza would be found there, later, and this story was now yet another the Philistines told to

Samson

one another. Awe mixed with fear in the hearts of the Philistines. Samson had done this! No one but Samson!

The hill above Hebron where the gate of Gaza was found was a two-day walk from Gaza!

Secret Code:

——	——	——	——	——
2-1-2-7	3-4-9-1	1-2-7-2	7-1-1-1	6-3-5-2

——	——	——	——	——
1-2-2-9	5-1-1-2	3-1-1-2	2-1-1-1	4-3-3-7

9
Betrayed!

The city of Gaza was a place of celebration today. News of great importance had spread quickly, and now people filled the streets. But this was not a holiday or a festival. The people had indeed come out today to rejoice, but also because they were curious. Was the news they had heard really true?

Yes, it was! The number one enemy of the Philistines was their prisoner. Samson was in chains! He was just now being led by his captors through the city streets.

Few of the people of the city cheered, however, as they watched Samson go by. The sight was shocking. Blood covered his face. He had been blinded! And his long black locks of hair had been chopped short. He stumbled along with his arms wrapped in bronze chains—a pitiful, drooping wreck of a human being.

But how? Everyone was convinced that Samson was invincible. What had happened?

Today there was much talk in Gaza.

"Betrayed," was the word. "By a woman!"

"But how? He was too strong to be overcome."

"Ah, but he had a weakness, it seems. His hair."

"His hair!"

"That was his secret. But it was cut, as you saw, and he is as weak as any mortal man."

"And the woman, why would she—?"

"Ha, ha, she is a rich woman now, I think."

It was in the Valley of Sorek that it happened. Samson had fallen in love with a woman there whose name was Delilah. She was a Philistine but with a Hebrew name. Samson, alas, had a weakness for women. And especially for women of heathen nations? Perhaps. Samson did not seem to care that these foreign women worshipped false gods and not the true God of his own people, Israel. Samson was a man of strong passions and a weak will. This weakness would be his ruin.

The Philistines were constantly looking for a way to

capture or kill Samson. They had spies who shadowed him wherever he went. They had found out about Delilah and had sent word to all five lords of the Philistine cities.

These lords themselves had gone to Delilah one night when she was alone.

"Would you like to be rich?" they asked her.

"What do you mean?" she asked.

"We want you to do something for us. It should be an easy thing, for you. If you can, you will be very, very rich."

"Tell me."

"We want you to get your lover, Samson, to tell you why he is so strong. It is said that there is some secret to his strength, that his power comes from his God—but that it can be taken away as well, somehow."

She was silent.

"You are a Philistine, remember," they said. "He is the enemy of our people—and he is not one of us. If you can do this, we will each give you one thousand and one hundred pieces of silver."

Her eyes went wide. "Each?" she said.

"Each! One thousand and one hundred pieces, each."

Samson

Samson and Delilah were alone together in her house. She stepped softly up to him and said, in her sweetest voice, "Tell me the secret of your strength. Tell me how you can be made as weak as any other man."

"Why?" he asked.

She put her arms around him. "Because I want to conquer you," she purred.

"But you have already done that."

She pouted. "Tell me."

He laughed. "All right. If I am bound with seven new bowstrings that are not dried out, I will be as weak as any other man."

And when Delilah was alone again, the Philistine spies came to her, and she told them about the bowstrings. They brought her seven new ones, just as she had told them. Now a group of Philistines would be hiding in the house next to Delilah's. And they would be watching, ready.

The next time Samson was with Delilah, she brought the bowstrings up to him and said playfully, "Now I am going to make you my prisoner."

He laughed and held out his arms, which she tied with the bowstrings. Then as Samson stood there grinning, she suddenly brought her hands to her mouth and gasped.

Samson

"Samson!" she cried. "Philistines, behind you!"

He snapped the bowstrings like threads and whirled around with a snarl. There was no one there. He turned to Delilah again, scowling. "Why did you deceive me?"

She frowned. "I deceived *you*? You lied to *me*! How can you say you love me when you won't tell me the truth? Now, please don't lie to me again. Tell me, how can you be made weak like other men?"

"If I am tied with new ropes that have never been used," Samson said.

And the next night they were together, Delilah tried this, just as before. And just as before, Samson snapped the ropes as easily as blades of grass when she cried, "Samson, the Philistines!"

The next time she tried the same thing, he told her, "If you weave my seven locks of hair into a loom and make it tight with a peg, I will be as weak as any other man."

Later that night, after Delilah had lulled Samson to sleep with rich food and much wine, she carefully tied his seven locks into a loom and made the knot fast with a peg. But this time, too, when she shouted, "The Philistines!" she knew he had lied again. He pulled his hair loose from the loom and leapt to his feet.

Then she buried her face in her hands and wept. "How can you say you love me when you do not mean it?" She sobbed. "You have made a fool of me three times. You have lied to me three times. All I want to know is what makes you so strong. And you won't even tell me!"

Samson's angry scowl softened. He sighed. "All right," he said. "But you must promise me—you must promise—that you will never tell my secret to anyone."

Delilah looked up through her tears. "I promise," she said. "How could you ever think I would do such a thing?"

"I am a Nazirite," Samson said. "This means my life is dedicated to God. My hair has never been cut from the time I was born. This is the sign of my dedication to God. And if my hair were cut, I would lose my strength."

Delilah knew (she could just tell) that Samson was telling the truth this time.

As soon as she was alone, she went to the Philistines hiding in the house next to hers and told them to be ready the next night.

And the next night she put her plan into action. Again, she lulled Samson to sleep, and as he lay there she snipped off the seven locks of his hair.

This time when she cried, "Samson, the Philistines!" and he jumped to his feet, the Philistines *were* there. Samson looked at them, then at Delilah, in shock. Then

Samson

the Philistines were on him. And Samson's strength was gone! The Philistines bound him in chains of bronze and put out his eyes.

And they brought him to Gaza and to the dungeon. And the great Samson, he who had killed many Philistines, was dragged down the stairs to the lowest part of the dungeon and chained to a grinding wheel. There, around and around in a circle he tread, day after day, grinding grain for his enemies' bread.

Secret Code:

___   ___   ___   ___   ___   ___
3-3-4-3 1-1-1-1   5-3-2-3 1-2-5-1 1-1-9-1 3-1-1-5

___   ___   ___   ___   ___   ___
6-1-5-2 5-3-4-6 2-1-5-8 2-8-1-2 1-1-4-1 5-1-5-2 6-3-1-1

10
Destruction of Dagon

Samson's world was now complete darkness. He plodded on and on, around and around in a circle, pushing on the wooden handle that turned the massive grinding stone. Day and night were the same to him now in his blindness. Time meant nothing to him. He only knew that he pushed the grinding wheel and that sometimes he was unchained from the handle and led by the hand to a pile of something that felt like straw on the cold, stone floor where he slept. Then he was shaken awake again and given bread and water and then chained to the wheel again.

This was all there was now. There was nothing else. To Samson, it could have been a day or it could have been an eternity.

But his thoughts were not chained, and his memory

was not blinded. He saw the vineyards he knew as a boy. He saw his father, his sturdy back bent over, his busy hands at work. And those eyes. His father's eyes were like pools of light. They were deep and clear and full of love. And Samson saw his mother, her kind face, the soft, tender look in her eyes as she smiled at him—as she so often had.

And he remembered what they had told him, about the angel of the Lord who had said Samson was to be dedicated to the Lord, that he was not to. . .to cut. . .his. . .

Delilah! Her face came to Samson often in his memories. Oh, how he wished it would not!

And there was that other Philistine woman, of Timnah, and the fire. . . .

Now Samson had nothing but memories, and the memories were nothing but bitterness.

And his thoughts? He had only one thought now. *Oh, if I could only die!*

But in this place, this dark, bitter place of pain and painful memories, this endless torment of plodding on and on in a circle, straining at the handle of the grinding wheel—there was something else. It was not there at first, not for a long, long time; but it came slowly, edging its way little by little into Samson's heart—past the bitterness, the hate, and the self-pity—until finally it had secured its own place in his heart. And now there was something new in Samson's life.

Repentance.

Although he was not even aware of the change in his heart, his memories were different now. He did not see so much of the things and the people who had caused him pain. Now, more and more, he saw the real source of his own hurt and failure. He saw his *Self*.

He himself had made his own choices in his life. He had lived as he pleased and done whatever he wished. He had given little thought to God and had hardly ever even considered the special call that God had placed on his life. He had prayed only once in his life, and that was only as he was about to die of thirst. (Samson did not realize, of course, that the Lord had used him, anyway, just as the Lord had intended, to strike the Philistines. Samson only realized that he himself had failed. He had sinned against his God and against himself. Samson knew now that only he was to blame for his ruined life, and no one else.)

Samson

The Philistines had gathered today in the huge temple of their god Dagon. All five lords of the Philistine cities were here, as well as some three thousand people of Gaza. The lords had decided to hold a celebration and to offer sacrifices to their god, who—so they said—had given them victory over their greatest enemy ever—Samson.

"Bring our prisoner here," the lords told the guards.

The guards sent a boy to the dungeon with a message for the prison guard to release Samson. The boy then led Samson by the hand to the temple.

"Look!" came the cries. "There he is, the great Samson! A boy leads him by the hand!"

"Come, Samson, perform for us!"

"Yes, show us some of the wonders we have heard of."

"Tell us, oh, great Samson, tell us the secret of your strength. Wonder of wonders, look how the boy strains to pull you about like a dog!"

The boy, of course, was not straining. Samson shuffled along awkwardly, docilely, behind the boy. Samson's head was bowed, his shoulders stooped.

The shouts and jeers of the crowd were deafening. Samson called now to the boy, "Please, boy, let me touch the columns that hold up the temple. I am weak. I need to lean on something."

These were the two great columns that held up the upper story and roof of the whole temple. This was the way the Philistines' temples and largest houses were built. The columns stood close together in the middle of the building.

The boy led Samson to these now. Samson put his hand out and felt one of them. He felt the air with his other hand until he touched the other column. The crowd was laughing with delight. What was this pantomime Samson was performing for them? Was he insane?

Samson stood between the columns with one hand on each. He bowed his head. "Sovereign Lord," he prayed, "please remember me. And, please, Lord, give me my strength just this one more time. Let me die with the Philistines."

Then Samson took a deep, deep breath. His back bowed; his shoulders bunched together.

Now the Philistines were delighted. What was Samson doing? This was better, much better, than they had hoped for. Their great enemy, the hero Samson, the ridiculous Samson, was indeed putting on a show for them. It was wonderful! The fool had lost his mind completely. He was between the columns, pushing against them like a madman straining to hold up the world.

C-r-a-c-k!

Suddenly there was silence. The laughter and the screaming and shouting had disappeared in an instant.

That sound had been unmistakable. It was an ear-splitting, grating sound that boomed out over the temple like thunder.

Now a shrieking gasp went up from the whole crowd. The columns were moving! Samson's face and neck were crimson from the strain as he pushed and pushed.

Then came another *crack!* and another grating *boom*, and the columns trembled and shook and buckled, and they came crashing down with an earthshaking roar. The roof and walls of the temple followed the columns like an avalanche, down, down, down.

The great temple of Dagon was a mountain of rubble, the tomb of all five of the lords of the Philistines and thousands of Philistines of Gaza—and of Samson.

In this one last act he had killed more of his enemies than he had in his whole lifetime.

Samson

In the book of Hebrews, in the eleventh chapter, many men and women of the Old Testament are listed in what is called the Hall of Faith. Samson's name is there, in Hebrews 11:32.

Not in his lifetime, not in his triumphs and victories, but only in the end, Samson found faith. How exactly it came to him we do not know. The story does not tell.

But the book in which is found the story of Samson *does* tell of faith.

> *Now faith is the substance of things hoped for, the evidence of things not seen. . . . Through faith we understand that the worlds were framed by the word of God, so that things which are seen were not made of things which do appear.*
> HEBREWS 11:1, 3

> *But now the righteousness of God without the law is manifested, being witnessed by the law and the prophets; even the righteousness of God which is by faith of Jesus Christ unto all and upon all them that believe: for there is no difference: for all have sinned, and come short of the glory of God; being justified freely by his grace through the redemption that is in Christ Jesus.*
> ROMANS 3:21–24

Samson

[Faith says that] the word is nigh thee, even in thy mouth, and in thy heart: that is, the word of faith, which we preach; that if thou shalt confess with thy mouth the Lord Jesus, and shalt believe in thine heart that God hath raised him from the dead, thou shalt be saved. For with the heart man believeth unto righteousness; and with the mouth confession is made unto salvation. . . . For whosoever shall call upon the name of the Lord shall be saved.
ROMANS 10:8–10, 13

Secret Code:

____ ____   ____ ____ ____
3-2-1-5 6-4-7-1   1-1-5-7 6-2-6-5 2-2-1-2

____ ____ ____ ____ ____
3-1-1-3 3-3-1-1 5-5-3-5 1-2-3-2 2-4-4-5

____ ____ ____ ____ ____ ____.
1-1-1-1 5-1-1-1 6-4-3-4 1-3-6-5 3-3-4-4 2-5-3-8

Young Reader's Bible Dictionary

Dagon: False god of the Philistines. Some old images show Dagon as half man and half fish. A statue of Dagon fell down and broke into pieces when the Philistines once put God's ark of the covenant into Dagon's temple (1 Samuel 5:1–4).

Faith: Confidence in something you've been told. Faith is another word for trust. Jesus said we must have faith in God (Mark 11:22), and that without faith, it is impossible to please God (Hebrews 11:6).

Israelites: God's chosen people. Also called "Hebrews" and "Jews," the Israelites were the extended family of Abraham and Sarah, through their grandson Jacob. Jacob once wrestled with the angel of God, who changed Jacob's name to "Israel" (Genesis 32:28).

Judahites: The extended family of Judah, the fourth son of Jacob. Judah led one of the "twelve tribes of Israel." In the time of the judges, this tribe tried to hand Samson over to the Philistines (Judges 15).

Judge: A term meaning "deliverer," a type of military leader in Israel. When God's people "did that which was right in [their] own eyes" (Judges 17:6), God allowed foreign countries to trouble Israel.

When the people cried out to God, He would send a judge—like Samson, Deborah, or Gideon—to battle Israel's enemies.

Moses: The man who led the Israelites out of their slavery in Egypt and wrote the first five books of the Bible. The Israelites look to Moses as their great prophet of God.

Nazirite: A person specially set apart to God. Nazirites made a special promise—"the Nazirite vow"—that said they would not drink alcohol or cut their hair for a period of time. Samson's Nazirite vow was for his whole life.

Philistines: One of Israel's main enemies. The Philistines lived in and around the "promised land" that God gave to Abraham and his descendants. They would fight the Israelites for many years. The giant Goliath, who fought young David, was a Philistine.

Repentance: A turning away from sin. The person who repents realizes sin is wrong and makes an effort to leave the sin behind. The apostle Paul said that God "commandeth all men every where to repent" (Acts 17:30).

YOUNG READERS
CHRISTIAN LIBRARY

Here are exciting Bible storybooks for 8 to 12-year-olds—Barbour's Young Readers' Christian Library! The stories of Jesus, Jonah, Esther, and Paul are carefully retold for kids, and illustrated with line art to help you envision the characters and setting of each story. And a special "secret code" feature adds fun—as you can discover an encouraging secret message woven throughout the entire book!

Wherever Christian books are sold.